Even Ninjas Have Nightmares

By: J.C. Roussos

DEDICATION

For all the people who are secret...
or not-so-secret...ninjas.

The monster comes for me, its skin slimy and purple and its arms reaching out to attack–

"Hi-yah!" I scream as I jump out of my bed.

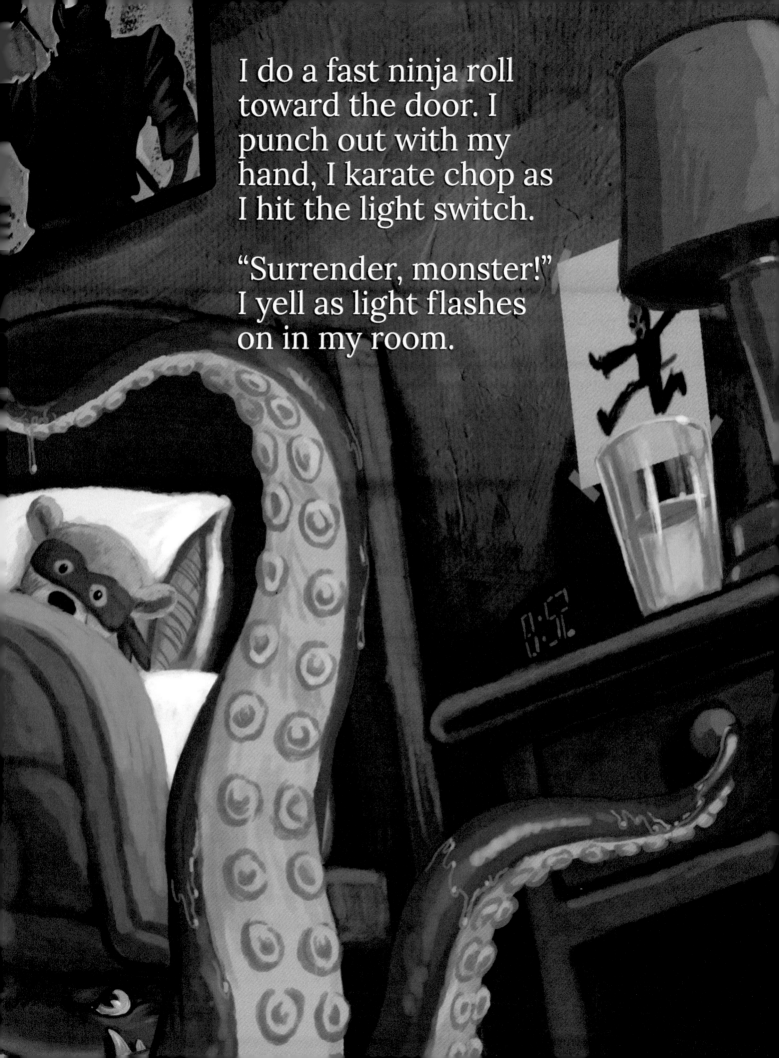

I do a fast ninja roll toward the door. I punch out with my hand, I karate chop as I hit the light switch.

"Surrender, monster!" I yell as light flashes on in my room.

But there is no monster there. No slimy-skinned monster with arms like an octopus.

My mom races into the room. "What's wrong?" she cries.

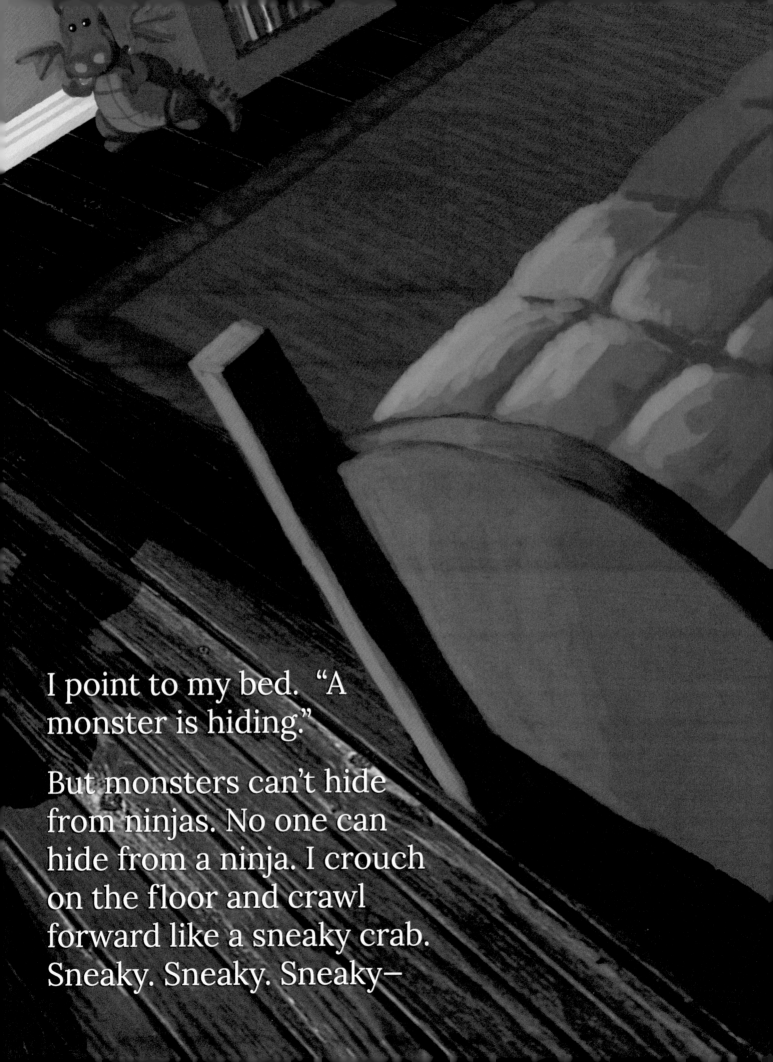

I point to my bed. "A monster is hiding."

But monsters can't hide from ninjas. No one can hide from a ninja. I crouch on the floor and crawl forward like a sneaky crab. Sneaky. Sneaky. Sneaky–

"Hi-yah!" I scream as I look under the bed. I see my old samurai sword. I see my ninja mask. I don't see a monster.

"Sweetie..." My mom sighs as she comes closer. "It's okay, even ninjas have nightmares."

I don't think it was a nightmare. I think it was a monster. One that is hiding now because he's afraid of the ninja. *That's smart, Mr. Monster. Hide while you can. The ninja is hunting you.*

My mom tucks me back into bed. "Go to sleep," she tells me. "You've got a big day in second grade tomorrow...and ninjas need their sleep."

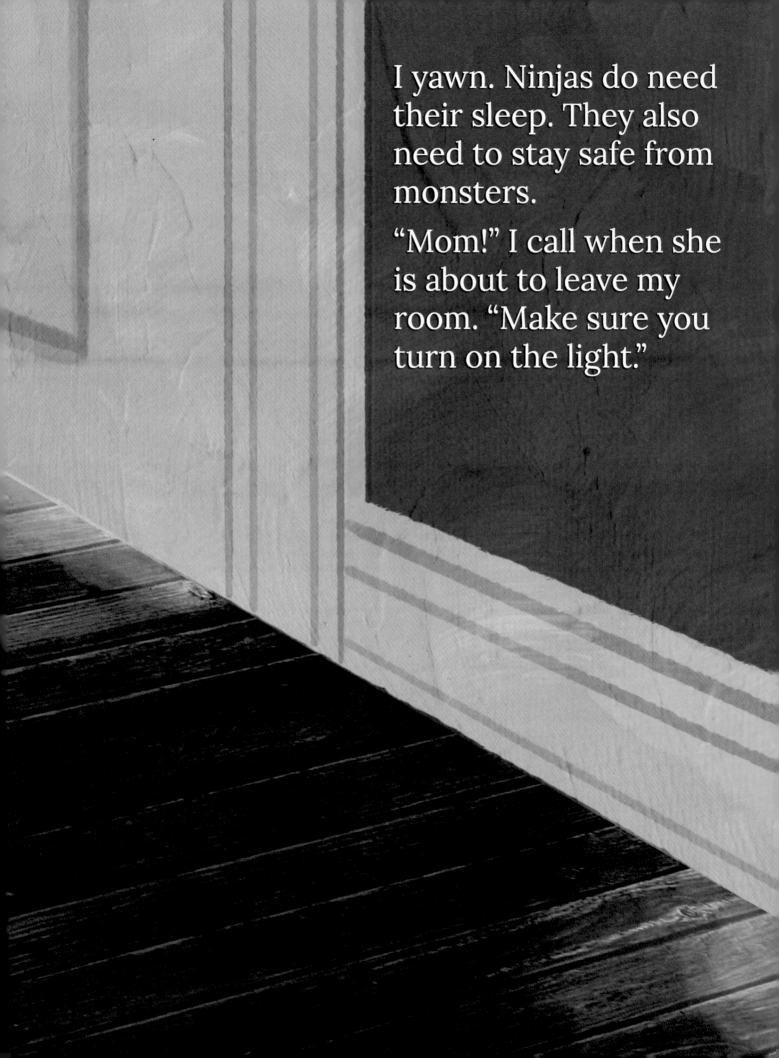

I yawn. Ninjas do need their sleep. They also need to stay safe from monsters.

"Mom!" I call when she is about to leave my room. "Make sure you turn on the light."

My ninja light. The ninja nightlight banishes the shadows. Now, if a monster comes at me, I'll see him.

I try to stay awake, but I slip back into my dreams. This time, no monsters are there. Probably because they're too afraid to face me.

The next night, I slide into the bed like a snake. Very softly.

Very s-s-s-ilently.

I don't want any monsters to know that I'm going to sleep. If they know I'm sleeping, they'll try to scare me.

My mom watches my snake-like moves. "It's okay to be afraid of nightmares," she tells me. "Everyone has them, even—"

"Ninjas aren't scared!" I tell her, and I jump up on the bed. Forget being silent. The monsters who wait in my dreams–or under my bed–need to fear the ninja.

I bounce, I kick, and I yell, "Hi-yah!" I am not a silent snake. I am a dancing dragon.

I will breathe fire and roar on my enemies. That octopus monster will never touch me!

"Got you!" Mom wraps her arms around me. "Ninja, it's time to sleep."

She tucks me in. Mom kisses my forehead, then she even gives me a little bow. Mom knows that's the way to tell a ninja good night.

When she starts to leave, though, I stop her. "Keep the door open," I tell her. "Just in case..."

And my mom does. She understands that ninjas always need to be prepared.

It's the scream that wakes me up. Loud, long, and scared. Someone is in trouble! *Ninja needed, ninja needed!*

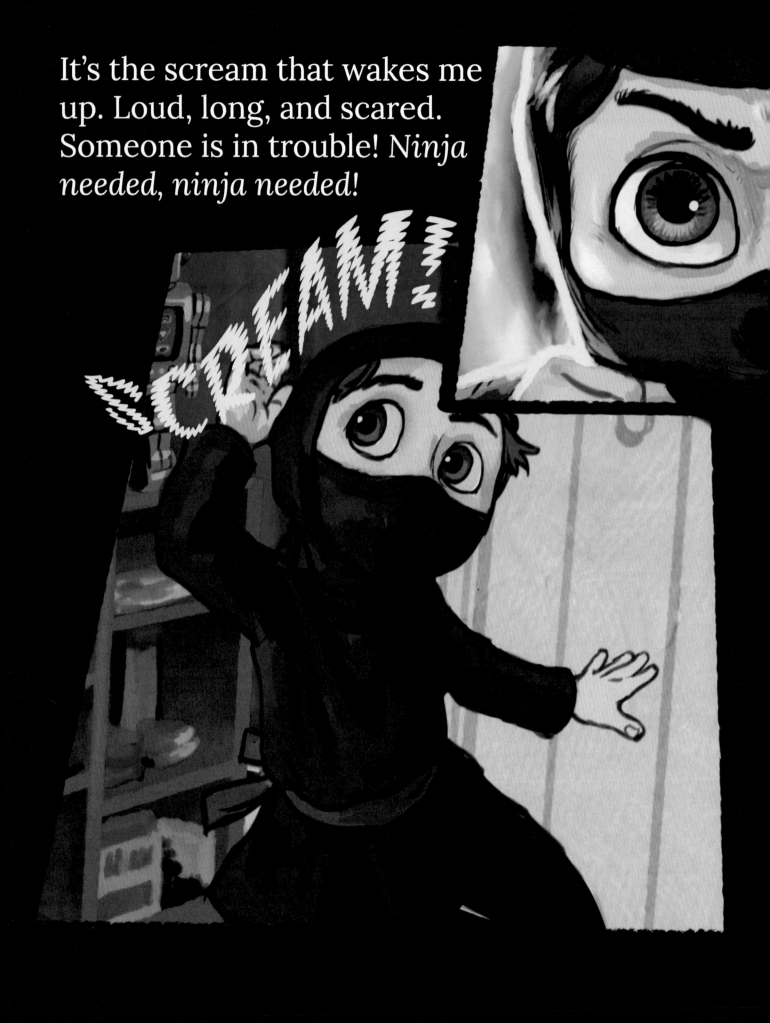

I run from my room and race down the hallway. I can still hear the scream—it is coming from my little sister's room. I kick open the door, *Hi-yah!*

"Ninja here!" I yell. "Monsters, beware!"

I punch to the left.
No monster is there.

I do a side kick to the
right. No monster
there, either.

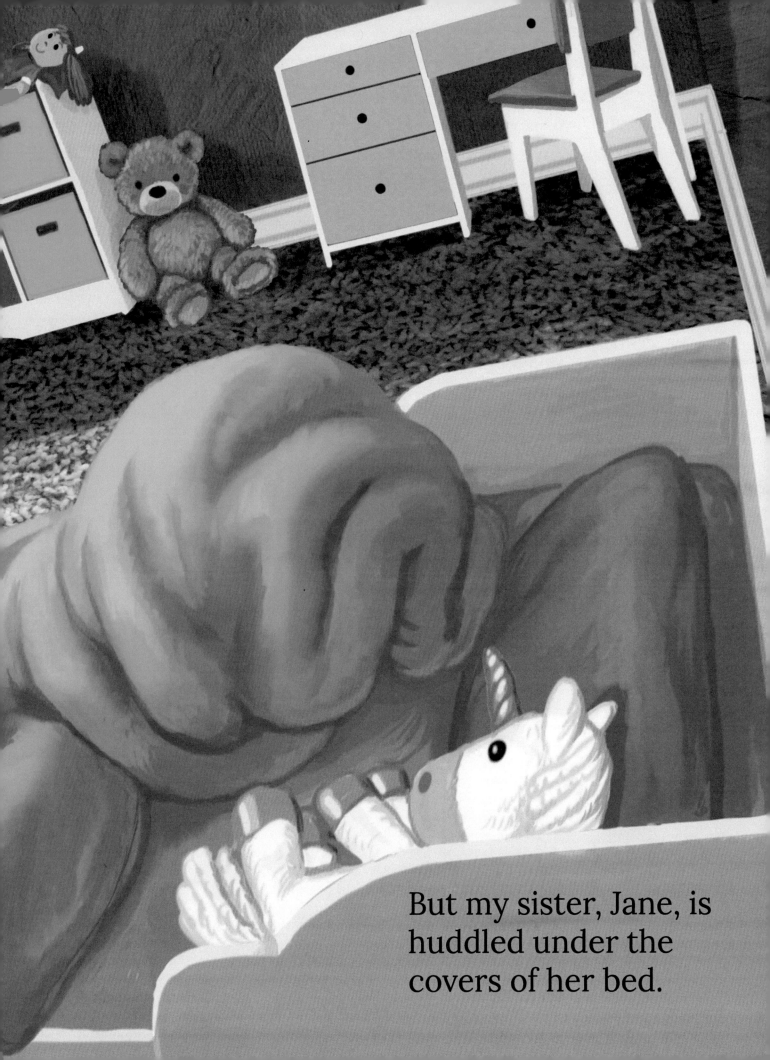

But my sister, Jane, is huddled under the covers of her bed.

The lights flash on, bright and strong. I glance back, ready to battle a monster—but it's just my mom, standing in the doorway.

"Bad dream, Jane?" Mom asks.

I look over and see Jane poke out her
head–turtle style–from beneath the mound
of covers. She nods. Her body shakes.

I rush to Jane's bed, galloping fast like a horse. I reach out, and I touch Jane's shaking shoulder. "It's okay," I tell her.

Jane glances up. Her eyes are wide and scared.

"Even ninjas have nightmares," I say.

Jane smiles.

I tuck Jane into bed. I kiss her forehead. Then I bow.

When Jane goes back to sleep, she's still smiling.

And when I go back to my room, I don't even bother glancing under the bed. I know I can handle any monster that comes my way. Any time, any day.

Because ninjas do have nightmares... but ninjas don't need to be afraid of nightmares.

ABOUT THE AUTHOR

J.C. Roussos is actually a mother and son writing team. The "J" is a black belt who loves video games, wizards, and reading. The "J" is a not-so-secret ninja. The "C" is a former teacher who spent years working with students who had learning differences. The "C" is also a *New York Times* and *USA Today* best-selling author under a different pen name.

ABOUT THE ILLUSTRATOR

Joe M. Ruiz is an artist whose illustrations can be seen in a number of children's books, board games, card games, and various illustrated manuscripts. He is the proud father of two of the greatest kids on the planet, and he lives a quiet life in Georgia with his awesome, patient and beautiful wife.

53500794R00020

Made in the USA
San Bernardino, CA
18 September 2017